Cookie Crisis!

by Sarah Willson
illustrated by Sharon Ross
and Shannon Bergman

SCHOLASTIC INC.

New York   Toronto   London   Auckland   Sydney
Mexico City   New Delhi   Hong Kong   Buenos Aires

K⬚**L**⬚**a**⬚**S**⬚**K**⬚**Y**
C⬚**S**⬚**U**⬚**P**⬚**O**⬚ ɪɴᴄ.

Based on the TV series *Nickelodeon All Grown Up!*™ created by Arlene Klasky,
Gabor Csupo, and Paul Germain as seen on Nickelodeon®

No part of this publication may be reproduced, stored in a retrieval system,
or transmitted in any form or by any means, electronic, mechanical,
photocopying, recording, or otherwise, without written permission of the
publisher. For information regarding permission, write to
Simon Spotlight, Simon & Schuster Children's Publishing Division,
1230 Avenue of the Americas, New York, NY 10020.

ISBN 0-439-76077-1

Copyright © 2004 by Viacom International Inc.
NICKELODEON, *All Grown Up*, and all related titles, logos, and characters are
trademarks of Viacom International Inc. Created by Klasky Csupo Inc.
All rights reserved. Published by Scholastic Inc.,
557 Broadway, New York, NY 10012, by arrangement with Simon Spotlight,
Simon & Schuster Children's Publishing Division. SCHOLASTIC and
associated logos are trademarks and/or registered trademarks of Scholastic Inc.

12 11 10 9 8 7 6 5 4 3 2 1   5 6 7 8 9 10/0

Printed in the U.S.A.   23

First Scholastic printing, September 2005

"Uh-oh," said Dil.

"I forgot to tell Mom about

our bake sale today."

"Aw, Dil," said Tommy.

"If we do not bring something,
  we might not have enough money
  for the dance on Friday!"

"No problem," said Dil.

"Mom probably has a box of

cookies in the kitchen."

They searched the cabinets.

Tommy found a cookie tin

that was nearly full.

"We can put these into a shoe box,"

he said to Dil.

"That way they will look homemade."

All the kids took turns selling

cookies during their lunch periods.

"I baked brownies," said Susie.

"My mom's chef baked
French pastries," said Angelica.
Quietly, Tommy put his shoe box
on the table in the back.

Vice Principal Pangborn came by

to see what was for sale.

"Mmm!" he said.

"I will buy two of those."

Vice Principal Pangborn took a bite.
"Yum!" he said. "There is nothing
quite like the taste of
home-baked cookies.

He pointed at the shoe box.

"Dil and Tommy made those,"

said Chuckie helpfully.

"Nice job, Pickles. I like to see students who know how to work for what they want."

Tommy smiled weakly.

Next period was Dil's turn to work.

Mr. Pangborn came back.

"Those cookies you baked

are terrific!" he said.

"They not only taste great—

they make me feel great.

I have more pep and energy

than I have had in years!"

He bought the whole box of them.

The bake sale was a success!

That afternoon Tommy and Dil

wanted a snack.

Tommy found the cookie tin.

"Those are not for you!" Didi said.

"I bought them for Spike—

Liver-Flavored Peppy Dog treats.

I put them in that tin because
he chewed up the bag.
They are supposed to give old dogs
extra pep and energy."

"We sold dog treats
to Mr. Pangborn,"
Tommy told his friends
the next day.
"He will be mad when he finds out,"
said Kimi.

"Maybe he will never find out,"

said Chuckie hopefully.

"PICKLES!" shouted a voice.

Tommy and Dil turned around.

It was Vice Principal Pangborn.

He loomed over Tommy and Dil.

"Those cookies of yours are amazing!"
the vice principal yelled.
"I have not felt this peppy
in years!"
Suddenly Mr. Pangborn's
beeper sounded.
"I want that recipe!"
he said before rushing off.

"We're toast," said Dil sadly.

"Hey, guys," said Kimi.

"Maybe we can figure out

how to make cookies

that look and taste

just like Spike's dog treats."

They made cookie dough.

They shaped it like the dog treats.

When the cookies were baked,

Phil took a bite.

He shook his head.

"They do not taste right," he said.

"Spike's treats are liver-flavored,"
   said Dil. "Maybe we should
   add some liver to the dough."

"Good idea," said Tommy.

"Let's go to the grocery store."

The friends hurried toward

the meat section.

Suddenly they heard a shout.

"Pickles!"

It was Vice Principal Pangborn!

It was too late to run.

Vice Principal Pangborn

had seen them.

"How about that recipe?"

he asked Tommy and Dil.

"Um, you see . . . ," Dil began.

"Our dog chewed it up!"
Tommy blurted out.

"Yeah!" said Dil. "And now
we cannot remember what was
in those cookies!"

"Well, too bad," said Mr. Pangborn.

"I sure did enjoy them. Say!"

He had just noticed a sign above

Tommy's head.

"If I did not know any better,

I would say those dog treats

look just like your cookies!"

He laughed loudly at the idea.

Kimi nudged Chuckie.

They laughed too.

Everyone had a blast at the dance.

And no one danced with more

pep and energy

than Vice Principal Pangborn.